13563

292
FIS

Fisher, Leonard
Everett

Theseus and the
Minotaur

$14.95

DATE			

THESEUS and the MINOTAUR

THESEUS
and the
MINOTAUR

WRITTEN AND ILLUSTRATED BY

LEONARD EVERETT FISHER

HOLIDAY HOUSE / NEW YORK

Leonard Everett Fisher consulted the following sources in retelling this ancient Greek myth:

Bullfinch, T. *Mythology*. New York: Random House Inc., Modern Library.

Ceram, C.W. *Gods, Graves, and Scholars*. New York: Alfred A. Knopf Inc., 1956.

Graves, R. *The Greek Myths*. volumes I & II, New York: George Braziller Inc., 1959.

Hamilton, E. *Mythology*. Boston: Little, Brown & Co. Inc., 1940.

Hawthorne, N. *The Greek Stories*. New York: Franklin Watts Inc., 1963.

Low, A. *Greek Gods and Heroes*. New York: Macmillan Publishing Co., 1985.

Copyright © 1988 by Leonard Everett Fisher
All rights reserved
Printed in the United States of America
First Edition

Library of Congress Cataloging-in-Publication Data

Fisher, Leonard Everett.
Theseus and the Minotaur.

Summary: Retells the Greek myth of the hero Theseus
and his battle with the bull-headed monster called the
Minotaur.
1. Theseus (Greek mythology)—Juvenile literature.
2. Minotaur (Greek mythology)—Juvenile literature.
[1. Theseus (Greek mythology) 2. Minotaur (Greek
mythology) 3. Mythology, Greek] I. Title.
BL820.T5F57 1988   398.2'2'0938   88-1970
ISBN 0-8234-0703-9

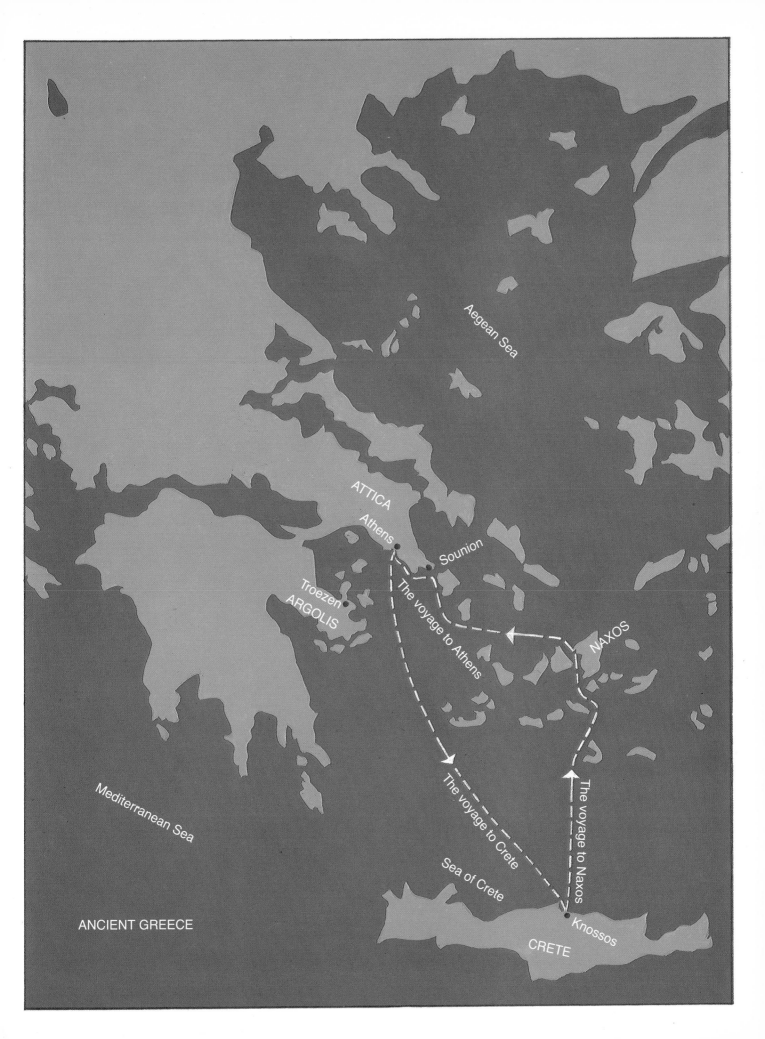

Aegean Sea

ATTICA
Athens
Sounion

Troezen
ARGOLIS

The voyage to Athens

NAXOS

Mediterranean Sea

The voyage to Crete

The voyage to Naxos

Sea of Crete

ANCIENT GREECE

Knossos

CRETE

Once upon a time a prince named Theseus was born in the city of Troezen. At the moment of his birth, his father, King Aegus of Athens, buried his favorite gold-hilted sword and sandals under a great rock.

"When Theseus is big and strong enough to move the rock, my sword and my sandals will be his," the king told Aethra, Theseus' mother. "Then and only then will Theseus be my heir and successor."

King Aegus returned to Athens. There he took a new wife, Medea, who bore him Medus, a second son.

Theseus grew up with his mother and grandfather. As a boy, he tried many times to move the rock. He strained with all his might and his face grew red, but the rock never budged. Finally, the day came when he was strong enough to push it away. There, glittering beneath, lay his father's sword and sandals.

"Use the sandals to walk in your father's footsteps," Aethra told her son. "And the sword to fight enemies and monsters."

"I must go to my father," said Theseus. "I shall make him proud of me."

"Then you must travel by sea," his grandfather advised, "since robbers might attack you on land."

"Don't worry, Grandfather," Theseus boasted. "I will take the road. My father's sandals will guide me, and his sword will protect me."

No sooner had Theseus set out on the road to Athens, than Procrustes, a cruel robber, blocked his way. Procrustes liked to tie his victims to a bed. He stretched out the people who were too short and lopped off the legs of those who were too tall. But Procrustes was no match for Theseus, who struck him down with his sword. Scinis and Sciron, two other robbers, met the same fate. From then on Theseus was hailed as a hero everywhere he went. No one knew that he was a prince. He was simply considered a daring youth who had made the road safe for travelers.

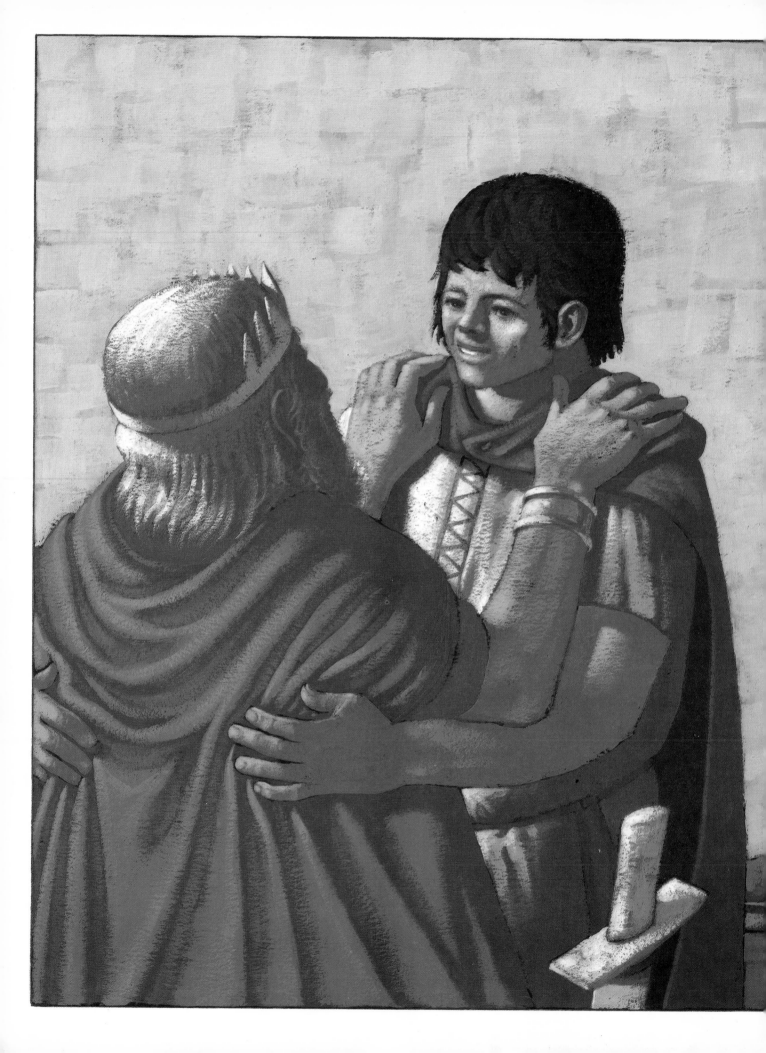

Hearing about the young man's bravery, his father, King Aegus, invited Theseus to a palace banquet in Athens. When Theseus arrived, the king did not recognize him. But Queen Medea's magic powers told her who he was. She knew, too, that if Aegus found out, Medus, her own son, would never be king. Theseus had to die! She convinced Aegus that Theseus would kill him, as he had the robbers, so he could take the throne for himself. Medea and Aegus plotted to have Theseus drink a cup of poisoned wine. As Theseus was about to take a sip, Aegus spied the sword dangling from his belt. He recognized it at once as the sword he had buried under the rock in Troezen long ago.

The old king knocked the cup from Theseus' hand and demanded to see his feet. "Your feet! Show me your feet!" Theseus obliged. "Those sandals!" the king shouted. "They were mine, too! You are Theseus my son! And you!" he cried, pointing to Medea, "you shall be punished for your trickery!" The king banished Medea and Medus to a cold land far, far east of Athens.

Then Theseus and Aegus fell into each other's arms. They celebrated all night.

As morning drew near, the weary king told Theseus of his troubles: "Years ago," Aegus began, "Androgeus, son of King Minos of Crete, died in Athens during the games. Enraged, Minos attacked and crushed us. Each year since then he has forced me to send him seven youths and seven maidens to be fed to the Minotaur. The Minotaur is a frightful beast—half man, half bull— a monster! Minos keeps it in a labyrinth beneath his palace at Knossos. Its dark passages are endless and confusing. No one escapes the labyrinth, not even the Minotaur. Soon I must send the fourteen. Pity them, and pity us to have to bear such burdens."

"Let me go as one of the youths," Theseus pleaded. "I shall free Athens of Minos and his monster forever! I shall slay the Minotaur. None of us will perish. We shall all escape the labyrinth and return alive!"

At first Aegus would not hear of the idea. He was certain that Theseus and his companions would die. But finally he agreed to the plan.

Several days later a tearful crowd stood at the water's edge to bid the unlucky fourteen farewell. The boat taking the youths to Crete tugged at her mooring. The oarsmen prepared to hoist a black sail telling of her sad journey.

"I shall wait for your return at Sounion," Aegus told his son. "On your way back, hoist a white sail if you are alive and your journey has been successful."

Theseus promised and boarded the boat. In less than an hour, she was a speck on the southern horizon.

A strong tide and wind quickly brought the boat to the Cretan shore. And just as quickly, her wretched passengers were taken from her decks and paraded before King Minos. Among those watching was Ariadne, Minos' beautiful daughter. When she saw Theseus her heart quickened. Instantly she fell in love with him and decided that he had to be saved from the Minotaur. But the guards discovered Theseus' gold-hilted sword under his cloak and took it away. They dragged him to a dungeon beneath the palace before Ariadne could plead for his life. Theseus' frightened companions soon followed.

"You will be the first to be eaten," Theseus was told by his jailers.

Later Ariadne slipped into Theseus' dark cell. She declared her love and said that she would find a way to free him.

"I am Theseus, son of King Aegus," Theseus exclaimed. "I have come to kill the Minotaur. I cannot escape with you now and leave my friends behind to suffer."

"Then I cannot let the Minotaur dine on either you or your friends," Ariadne whispered. "Here, I've stolen your sword. Slay the monster. Take this ball of silk thread, too. You shall need it to find your way out of the labyrinth. Lose it and you will be lost forever. Guard it well. Daedalus, the man who built the labyrinth, told me it was the surest and only way out of the winding passages. I shall hold one end of the thread as you unwind the ball. Follow the thread back to me, and you will escape."

Ariadne and Theseus sneaked past the sleeping guards and reached the labyrinth entrance. Ariadne held on to one end of the thread as Theseus disappeared into the gloom.

Theseus saw a dim glow ahead of him. A far-off throaty rumble rolled through the labyrinth like distant thunder. The ground shook as dirt and pebbles slid from the damp stone walls. Theseus wound his way toward the glow, unraveling the silk thread as he went. Water drips echoed around him. He gripped his sword as he heard another rumble. The ground shook again. Theseus moved to his right, then to his left as the labyrinth twisted and turned. After a while he found himself in the center of a large space lit by torchlight. Human bones and skulls littered the ground. Suddenly a great shadow darted across the wall. A loud bellowing roar split the dank air close behind him. Once more the ground shook. Theseus froze where he stood. The ball of silk thread fell to the ground. Now crouching and holding his sword with both hands, Theseus slowly turned to face the Minotaur—half man, half bull—all beast!

With its huge head lolling from side to side, the Minotaur began to circle Theseus. It snorted and reached for him, but Theseus leaped to the side. Quickly he backed away from the beast, holding his sword straight out before him. Again the snorting Minotaur attacked. It lowered its head and charged, hoping to pin Theseus to one of its great horns. But Theseus dodged the attack and came up behind the huge beast, chopping a blow that drew blood from the Minotaur's shoulder. Bellowing with surprise, the Minotaur whirled and charged again. Theseus sidestepped the bawling monster as he struck it a mighty swiping blow across its lower legs. The Minotaur dropped to its knees, still reaching for Theseus, and rolled over onto its back, groaning with pain. In an instance Theseus was upon the Minotaur and drove his sword home. The Minotaur shuddered and died.

Theseus had saved himself and his companions. He found the ball of silk thread and easily made his way back to the waiting Ariadne.

"It is done!" he cried. "The Minotaur is dead!"

"Be quiet," whispered Ariadne. "You will wake the guards, and we shall not be able to escape."

Then she added, "My father will never forgive me for what I have done. Let me go with you to Athens. We shall be married there." The grateful Theseus agreed.

Theseus and Ariadne freed the thirteen young Athenians. They all fled in the night to the safety of the boat that brought them. They released the lines and silently rowed away from the shore. The black sail caught a breeze, and those on board rowed with the wind toward Athens.

The boat took a course slightly to the northeast that brought them to the island of Naxos. Being hungry and thirsty—the boat had no food, water, or wine—they searched the island for something to eat and drink. They found plenty of everything, and everyone feasted. Having had their fill of meats, berries, nuts, and wine, Theseus and Ariadne fell asleep.

As Theseus slept, Dionysus, son of Zeus and God of Wine, entered his dreams. Dionysus told Theseus that he had long loved Ariadne and wished to marry her; and that if he, Theseus, knew what was good for him, he would depart from the island immediately and leave Ariadne to him, the god, Dionysus.

Theseus awoke with a start. He awakened his companions, gathered them aboard the ship and sailed for Athens. Ariadne was left to the love of Dionysus.

Theseus never truly recovered from his terrible mistake. Had he not forgotten to hoist the white sail, his father would have known that he was alive and that he would no longer have to worry about the cruelties of King Minos.

Theseus became the hero-king of Athens. But not long after, he stepped down from the throne. He thought that the people would be better off ruling themselves than to be ruled by one king. For the rest of his life, he was much loved by everyone. Athenians can still be heard saying, "Nothing without Theseus."

Theseus was upset as he thought of his love for Ariadne. He had wanted to marry his princess, but a god—Dionysus—had spoken. Theseus may have been strong and clever enough to kill the hideous Minotaur, yet he had not been strong and clever enough to outwit a god.

In his misery Theseus forgot to exchange the black sail for a white one. King Aegus, patiently waiting at Sounion for his return, spotted the boat with her black sail.

The old king sent a mournful cry across Sounion. The message of the black sail was clear and unmistakable: Theseus was dead! The Minotaur had destroyed him along with the unlucky thirteen! The king ran to the edge of the cliff and flung himself into the sea below, where he drowned. From that moment the sea was called the "Aegean Sea."